The Stone Cutter

A story from Japan
retold by Sean Taylor
illustrated by Serena Curmi

Collins

A poor stone cutter
chipped at a rock.
His hammer went TACK
and his chisel went TOCK.

Then a rich man walked past,
in his rich man's clothes.
"I'm just a poor stone cutter,"
the stone cutter said.
"I'd rather be a rich man instead."

And he became a rich man.

Then the emperor rode past with his servants dressed in blue and gold.

"I'm just a rich man," the stone cutter said.
"I'd rather be the emperor instead."

And he became the emperor.

Then the sun came out.
It was grander and more powerful
than any emperor.

"I'm just an emperor," the stone cutter said.
"I'd rather be the sun instead."

And he became the sun.

Then a big cloud passed.
It blocked out all the sun's light.
"I'm just the sun," the stone cutter said.
"I'd rather be a cloud instead."

12

And he became a cloud.

Then a wild wind blew the cloud
away across the sky.
"I'm just a cloud," the stone cutter said.
"I'd rather be the wind instead."

And he became the wind.

The wind blew until
it smacked into a huge rock.
"I'm just the wind," the stone cutter said.
"I'd rather be a rock instead."

16

And he became a rock.

Then he felt a poor stone cutter
chipping at his side.
"I'm just a rock," the stone cutter said.
"I'd rather be a poor stone cutter instead."

And he became a poor stone cutter once again.

The poor stone cutter
chipped at the rock.
His hammer went TACK
and his chisel went TOCK.

TACK

TOCK

The stone cutter

⁘ Ideas for guided reading ⁘

Learning objectives: To identify and describe characters, expressing own views; discuss and compare key themes; use word endings ('ed') in reading; respond to presentations by describing characters, highlights and commenting constructively.

Curriculum links: Citizenship: Choices

Interest words: chipped, walked, dressed, passed, blocked, turned, smacked, ordinary, chisel, emperor, servants, powerful

Word count: 283

Resources: Whiteboards and pens

Getting started

This book can be read over two sessions.

- Play the game 'scissors, paper, stones' (hand shape game where scissors cut paper, paper wraps stone, stone blunts scissors). Discuss what is happening in the game: that each element is more powerful than another, and weaker than another.

- Introduce the book to the children, looking at the cover and the blurb, and eliciting the fact that it is a traditional story from Japan.

- Read pp1–9. Children can follow the text with their eyes or finger as appropriate. Using group discussion, establish why the stone cutter wanted to be a rich man and then the emperor. Ask the children to predict what is going to happen next in the story.

- Ask the children if the story reminds them of any other stories. Ask the children if they have ever wanted to be something/one else. How does it feel?

Reading and responding

- Model how to approach a challenging word. Using the example 'ordinary' (p3), model using: graphic knowledge to search for words within words; use of phonological awareness to stretch and sound out phonemes; use of context to predict the word; use of the sentence grammar to predict the word.